STORIES

MEET THE CHARACTERS

SPIDEY

A SPECIAL SPIDER GAVE **PETER PARKER** SUPER POWERS. NOW HE **FIGHTS VILLAINS** AS SPIDEY!

MILES MORALES

MILES MORALES IS ALWAYS READY TO LEAP INTO ACTION. HE CAN TURN **INVISIBLE!**

GHOST-SPIDER

GWEN STACY IS SUPER SMART. AS GHOST-SPIDER, SHE CAN **GLIDE** ON HER **WEB WINGS.**

AUTUMN
PUBLISHING

Published in 2024
First published in the UK by Autumn Publishing
An imprint of Igloo Books Ltd
Cottage Farm, NN6 0BJ, UK
Owned by Bonnier Books
Sveavägen 56, Stockholm, Sweden
www.igloobooks.com

© 2024 MARVEL

0124 001
2 4 6 8 10 9 7 5 3 1
ISBN 978-1-83795-130-7

Cover designed by Charles Wood-Penn
Edited by Luke Robertson

Printed and manufactured in China

GREEN GOBLIN

GREEN GOBLIN **PLAYS TRICKS!** HE FLIES ON A GOBLIN GLIDER AND THROWS **PUMPKIN** PRANKS.

DOC OCK

DOC OCK IS VERY SMART. SHE WANTS TO **TAKE OVER THE CITY** WITH HER **METAL TENTACLES.**

RHINO

RHINO IS **BIG AND STRONG.** HE LIKES TO RUN AND **BREAK THINGS.**

HOW TO READ A COMIC

Follow our easy guide, and you will be reading comics in no time!

1 EACH PAGE OF A COMIC IS MADE UP OF PICTURES, OR **PANELS**. EACH PANEL TELLS ONE PART OF THE STORY.

2 THE CHARACTERS SPEAK IN WORD BALLOONS. THE POINTER OR TAIL AT THE END OF THE **BALLOON** SHOWS WHO IS SPEAKING.

3 SOMETIMES YOU WILL SEE WORDS IN A BOX. THAT IS CALLED A **CAPTION**. CAPTIONS HELP TELL THE STORY AND ADD THINGS YOU NEED TO KNOW, LIKE TIME OR LOCATION.

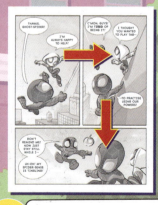

4 READ THE PANELS FROM LEFT TO RIGHT AND TOP TO BOTTOM. FOLLOW THE ARROWS ABOVE, AND YOU WILL SEE WHAT WE MEAN.

5 NOW SWING ON AND READ!

MEET THE HEROES!

MILES AND GWEN ARE HANGING OUT WITH PETER IN HIS ROOM.

WANT TO SEE MY DRAWING, GWEN?

YOU KNOW I DO, MILES!

BUT PETER GETS A SPIDEY-ALERT.*

TRACE-E **NEEDS** US!

LET'S GO TO THE WEB-QUARTERS!*

THE SECRET ENTRANCE IS THIS WAY!

IT'S SPIDEY TIME!

THE ADVENTURE BEGINS!

AT THE CINEMA!

I CAN'T WAIT TO SEE THIS FILM!

WHERE IS PETER?

MEANWHILE...

I AM LATE!

IF I DON'T HURRY...

... I WILL **MISS** THE FILM!

HELP!

THE END!

WHERE'S MILES?

MILES IS INSIDE THE WEB-QUARTERS.

HI, TRACE-E! SPIDEY AND GHOST-SPIDER ARE **LOOKING** FOR ME.

BUT I WILL PLAY A **JOKE** AND HIDE...

... WITH MY CLOAKING POWER!*

THE END!

OCTO-PALS!

LOOK, IT'S **CAL!**

CAL BELONGS TO **DOC OCK.**

DOC OCK MUST BE HERE SOMEWHERE.

SHE IS **ALWAYS** UP TO NO GOOD!

THERE IS NOWHERE TO RUN, CAL!

TEAM TIME!

OUR HEROES ARE WATCHING THE **DOG DAY PARADE!**

I CAN **GLIDE** TO CATCH HIM!

GIVE THOSE BALLOONS BACK!

BUT GREEN GOBLIN **DODGES!**

HAVE A PUMPKIN **PRANK*** INSTEAD!

I MISSED HIM!

BOOM

AND I GOT ANOTHER BALLOON!

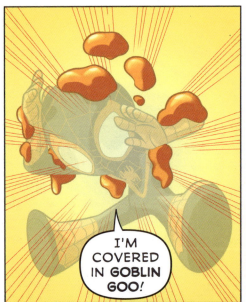

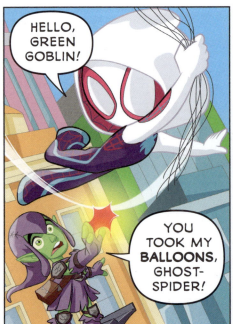

HELLO, GREEN GOBLIN!

YOU TOOK MY **BALLOONS**, GHOST-SPIDER!

THOSE AREN'T **YOUR** BALLOONS!

NOW I DON'T HAVE ANY BALLOONS.

THWIP

MAYBE A BALLOON WILL CHEER GREEN GOBLIN UP!

HERE YOU GO!

STOPPING BAD GUYS...

...AND CRAWLING WALLS...

... TEAM SPIDEY DOES IT **ALL**!

IT IS MY FAVOURITE COLOUR!

THE END!

RHINO RACE!

THE BIG LIBRARY PRANK!

THERE IS TROUBLE AT THE **LIBRARY**!

CAN YOU **HELP**, SPIDEY TEAM?

WHAT IS THE **TROUBLE**?

COME INSIDE...

... AND YOU WILL SEE!

LET'S GO!

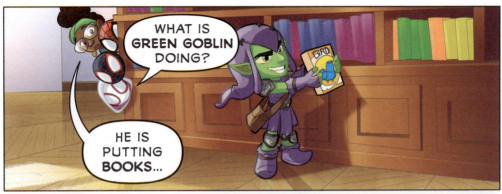

THE END!

MEET BLACK PANTHER!

SPIDEY EXPLAINS.

CAN YOU HELP GET BOOTSIE BACK?

BOOTSIE THINKS THIS IS A GAME.

WELCOME BLACK PANTHER

MAYBE BOOTSIE WILL COME TO **US**...

... IF I TRY **THIS!**

MEOW!

IT WORKED!

TO CATCH A CAT...

... YOU MUST **THINK** LIKE A CAT!

MEOW!

THE END!

SUPER HERO TEAM-UP!

DOC OCK IS UP TO NO GOOD.

I AM GOING TO TURN THIS **PARK** INTO ONE BIG **FISH TANK!**

IT WILL BE A KINGDOM FIT FOR AN **OCTOPUS!**

WE NEED SOME **HELP!**

TAP!

MEANWHILE, IN THE **WEB-QUARTERS...**

TRACE-E! COME IN, TRACE-E!

BEEP!

ONE QUICK CALL LATER...

THWIP!

WE NEED TO KEEP EVERYONE SAFE...

THANKS!

UNTIL HELP GETS HERE!

THE END!